The Old Man and the Fiddle

written and illustrated by

MICHAEL McCURDY

G. P. Putnam's Sons • New York

G. P. Putnam's Sons, a division of The Putnam & Grosset Book Group,
200 Madison Avenue, New York, NY 10016. Published simultaneously in Canada
Printed in Hong Kong by South China Printing Co. (1988) Ltd.
Book design by Gunta Alexander

Library of Congress Cataloging-in-Publication Data
McCurdy, Michael.   The old man and the fiddle / by Michael McCurdy.
p.   cm.   Summary: An old man insists on playing his fiddle without stopping,
as his house collapses around him and his neighbors complain.
[1. Violin—Fiction.   2. Neighborliness—Fiction.   3. Stories in rhyme.]
I. Title. PZ8.3.M139701 1992 [E]—dc20 90-23104 CIP AC
ISBN 0-399-21812-2
10 9 8 7 6 5 4 3 2 1
First Impression

To Christophe and Laurent Matson

There was an old man who liked to sit
On his shabby old porch with his little dog Kit.
He fiddled a tune he loved to hear—
A happy old tune that he played by ear.

His house was a shambles, the porch almost gone,
The yard was a sight, but the man fiddled on.

Neighbors came by and looked on in disdain,
The old man just winked and played a refrain:

Sunshine, moonshine, rainbow and cloud,
Everything's right when the music is loud.

"Your yard is a mess—I might injure my toe!"
Said Mr. McFee as he grabbed the man's bow.
The man grabbed it back, for he didn't mind.
His junk was his treasure, his mess was just fine!

"And what of your well?" asked little Miss Gish.
"It's full of tadpoles and slimy fish."
Instead of an answer the old man played louder,
Scratching his strings while sipping his chowder.

He didn't notice the pig in the tree,
The cat in the porridge, the hen drinking tea.

"Why not mend your roof?" asked Mrs. McKay,
The old man replied, "It's not raining today!"

The carpenter tried to patch up the roof,
But he fell through, right onto Mrs. Maloof.

The old man just smiled and tapped his heel,
Tightened his bow and continued his reel:

Sunshine, moonshine, rainbow and cloud,
Everything's right when the music is loud.

The tailor tried to cut the strings,
But he couldn't get close to the screechy things.
The cow danced a waltz, the pig did too,
The cat sang aloud, the hen ballyhooed.
"Stop!" cried the neighbors, all in a stew.
"This dreadful noise simply won't do!"

A farmer bribed him with geese and a swan,
A wagon and horse—but the man played on.

The baker offered him thirteen pies,
But the animals ate them before his eyes.

Then, in a flash, the sky turned gray,
The wind came and blew the hen away.
And all at once it rained so hard,
That raindrops quickly flooded the yard.

The man didn't mind, he continued to play.
Rain poured through the roof. His dog washed away.

Sunshine, moonshine, rainbow and cloud,
Everything's right when the music is loud.

Soon the house was afloat, along with the mess,
The cow, the pig and all the rest.
"Quick, save the house!" shouted Mr. Magee.
"Get hammers, get rope, and follow me!"

But the storm proved too mighty, the water too swift.
The house snapped the rope and started to drift.
It swirled, it bounced, it seemed very light,
It bumped, it careened, it sailed out of sight.

"Let that be a lesson!" cried Mr. McFee,
Grabbing the dog as he climbed up a tree.
"We warned him he should fix his roof!"
Shouted the elderly Mrs. Maloof.

Then the water subsided. The sky turned blue.
And the neighbors heard a sound they all knew.

The sound of a fiddle—it gave them a chill,
It rose from the valley, beyond the next hill!
Sunshine, moonshine, rainbow and cloud,
Everything's right when the music is loud.